SUPER MARIO™

MEET MARIO!

by Malcolm Shealy

Random House 🏠 New York

MARIO

Here We Go!

Mario is a cheerful person
who is no stranger to adventure
in the Mushroom Kingdom.
The Mushroom Kingdom
is a peaceful place.
But when there's trouble,
Mario can be counted on
to save the day!

LUIGI

Okey Dokey!

Luigi is Mario's
friendly brother.
Luigi tries to be brave,
but he is timid—
and afraid of ghosts!
Even so, he is willing
to join his brother on
any adventure.

DONKEY KONG

Going Bananas!

Donkey Kong is known
for his great strength
and red tie.
Bananas are Donkey Kong's
favorite food.

YOSHI

Big Appetite! *GULP!*

Yoshi is laid-back
and likes to eat fruit.
He helps Mario
by using his long tongue
to gobble up enemies.
He can flutter his legs
to jump really high
and avoid danger.

TOAD

Toad Time!

Toad is one of the citizens
of the Mushroom Kingdom.
He is loyal, cheerful,
and polite.
He's always happy to help
Princess Peach
whenever he's needed.

PRINCESS PEACH

Perfectly Peachy

Peach is the princess of the Mushroom Kingdom. She tries many things, including adventuring, sports, and kart racing.

DAISY

Princess Power

Daisy is the princess
of Sarasaland.
She is full of energy.
She also enjoys playing sports
and kart racing.

ROSALINA

Mysterious Friend

The mysterious Rosalina
came from outer space with
little Luma, the lost star child.
With her powerful star wand,
Rosalina is always calm
in the face of danger.

TOADETTE

Happy and Hardworking

Toadette lives in the Mushroom Kingdom. She is brave and always ready for adventure.

21

BOWSER

KING KOOPA

Mario's biggest and baddest foe
is Bowser.

With his pointy horns,

his fiery red hair,

and the spiky shell on his back,

Bowser is also the mighty

King Koopa!

BOWSER Jr.

Like Father, Like Son

Bowser Jr. is Bowser's energetic son.
He wears a bandanna painted
to look like a monstrous mouth.
He thinks it makes him look older!
Bowser Jr. is mischievous
and more than a little naughty.

KOOPALINGS

The Koopa Crew

Armed with magic wands
and other powerful weapons,
the Koopalings are trusted
and devoted helpers
of Bowser.

Wendy

Morton

Lemmy

Iggy

Roy

Ludwig

Larry

Their names are Lemmy, Wendy,

Morton, Iggy, Roy, Ludwig, and Larry.

Wherever there's a disturbance,

the Koopalings are

almost always involved!

MINIONS

Mighty Minions!

Only Bowser's mighty minions
stand between him and Mario.
Bowser's minions can be found
everywhere—marching in fields,
hiding in pipes, and even
swimming underwater!

Koopa
Troopa

Spiny

Kamek

Piranha Plant

Lakitu

Goomba

29

Bowser may be a lot of trouble,

but Mario's friends

gain courage

and stand up to Bowser

when they hear

Mario say . . .